HUMOUR, HEART AND HOPE
LIFE IN RHYME

Paul Dennison

© Copyright (2025) by (Paul Dennison) – All rights reserved.

It is not legal to reproduce, duplicate or transmit any part of this document in either electronic means or printed format. Recording of this publication is strictly prohibited.

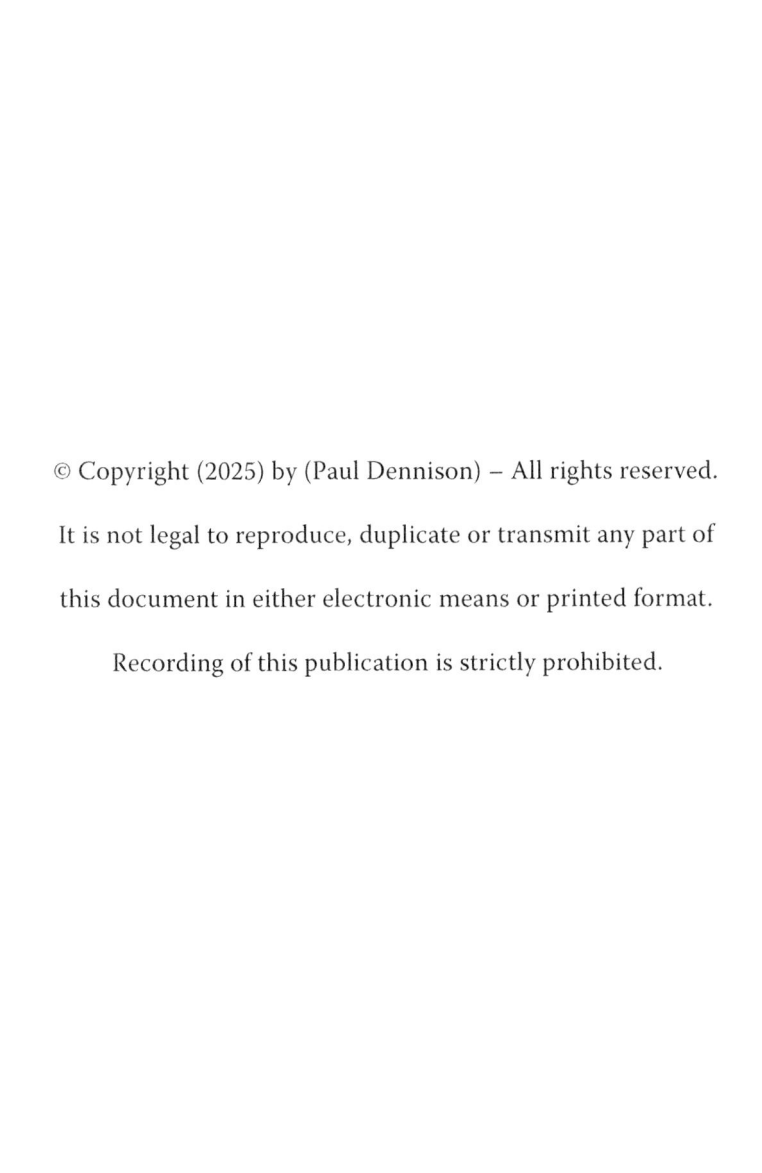

This book is dedicated to:

My Wife, Sharon, who has spent the last 4 years helping with my ongoing health condition's which are day to day, Thank you, I love you.

And to our Fantastic NHS – A heartfelt thank you!

Authors Note

Hi, I'm Paul, thank you for considering this book.
I loved writing these poems, once I got the hook.

I've never been a writer and not one for punctuation.
I can't spell, but told, I'm good at communication.

I have Parkinson's, a stoma and other health conditions.
When there's nothing in the tank, that's
when poems get additions.

Paul Dennison

These poems are varied, some made me cry.

They are all constructed in my mind, but the images are AI

Some Poems observational and some reflective

History, fantasy, and humour, complete the collective

Some of the contents are quite personal and come from within

We all battle with health conditions, so I thought I'd let you in

Introduction

Thank you for taking the time.

To read my poems that all rhyme

There written with a comedy tweak.

Derek, the donut is one you should meet.

There's a dementia poem, Bob1 & 2

Based on a real-life story to give you a clue

My latest ditty is about emotions, but with a twist.

Historical poem, quarter passed 2, yes, it's Henry the 5th.

Also available is kitchen Karnage, golf and the evasive sleep.

There's even one about Death, if that's not to deep

Later listings are Yellow Peril, IT and of course biscuits

Along with a few more comedy poems, should you risk it!

I hope you enjoy reading life in Rhyme

Humour, Heart and Hope you find the time

Foreword

In 2018, I was diagnosed with Parkinson's, it wasn't a shock as there was clearly something wrong, what did surprise me was how Anxiety just totally took over and left me isolated and unable to deal with people We know now that stomach health and Parkinson's are linked and in 2020, I developed severe ulcerated Colitis which drained my health,

I spent the next 9-months on the toilet and unable to venture out without the aid of a nappy and was heavily reliant on steroids, during this period I had various infusions and contracted Pneumonia which was my first stay in hospital. There were lots of scans in an effort to find out what was wrong, later that year, I had a stoma operation which went a little pear shaped, A bad reaction to all my Parkinson's and colitis meds, I spent 5 weeks in hospital, my Stoma finally decided it wanted to join in, and I was happily discharged.

*One month later I had a blockage, in for
emergency surgery, my stoma had twisted.
My second op went well but my recovery took much longer,
another 5 weeks in hospital and I was extremely ill.*

*When I finally got home, I had dropped to 8
stone, couldn't sleep and my operation had gone
septic, this had me bedridden for another month
– I had daily visits from the district nurses
I'd also developed a lung condition having contracted
pneumonia and an eye condition called Uveitis,
when I finally got back on my feet two months later
and able to leave the house, I contracted Covid*

*In hindsight catching covid turned out to be lucky, the
vaccination jabs work well and although ill, I was no
worse than most people, this gave me the confidence
to get out there and mix and get on with my life*

*These Poems are about my health Journey through
the last few years, the journey has been a battle*

Humour, Heart and Hope Life in Rhyme

but one I will approach in a positive manner, and hope these poems help others as they have me. In most circumstances there are comedy moments which lighten the mood, I hope these come across in this section Chapter One – 1-13, covers my Parkinson's, anxieties and my stoma

I'm here due to the care and attention from the NHS - #Heroes

Contents

Authors Note v
Introduction vii
Foreword ix

Chapter 1 - Parkinson's

1. Emotion's 1
2. I have a suit malfunction, Sir! 4
3. Shit happens 7
4. Stanley 10
5. Coping 13
6. Sleep – Insomnia 16
7. Food – Yes Please 19
8. Imagination 22
9. Golf – Will I Make it. 24
10. Kiss and Tell 29
11. The Board 32
12. Empty Shell, Do Tell 35
13. Inspiring 38

Chapter Two – Dementia

14. Bob One 45
15. Bob 2 49
16. Bob 3 52
17. If not yes, then Why 56
18. The Dementia Waltz 58

Chapter 3 – Grief

19. NUMB 61
20. What? Now? 63
21. The Hard Yards 66

Chapter 4 – Life in Rhyme

22. Quarter Passed Two 69
23. It's in the Diary 72
24. World War 3 75
25. Biscuits 78
26. Pete the Pothole 80
27. Pam-boos 83
28. Derek is a Donut 86
29. The Eternity Ring 91
30. A Poem for Poems 93
31. The Great Escape 95
32. 1066 – Oh, What a Month 97
33. Karnage in the Kitchen 100
34. I.T. 103
35. All That Jazz 106
36. Yellow Peril 109
37. Frozen in Time 111
38. It's only a word …. Death 115

Chapter 1 - Parkinson's

1. Emotion's

Emotions can be 3 different things that fit in rather snugly.

There is of course the good, the bad and the damn right ugly.

The good is the best emotion you can feel.

Adrenaline filled veins; the elation is real.

Paul Dennison

It can make you laugh, sing, and cheer.

While making everyone else seem very sincere

This is the emotion that we like the best.

It's a memory maker and you can keep the rest.

The next emotion is the one we call bad.

Has lots of connotations that can make you mad?

Lots of tears, just let it all out.

Makes you feel better without a doubt.

Dwelling on things is also sad.

Which also comes under the banner of bad?

The final one is just ugly and not really a friend.

The red mist descends, who is this bellend?

This emotion could get a lot worse.

But we're moving on for the sake of this verse.

All these emotions share similar groups.

Shouting, crying and others to boot

Humour, Heart and Hope Life in Rhyme

The Bad and Ugly are quite good mates.

They team up together and sometimes date.

In unison they can attack at anytime

Be positive and recognise these signs.

To tackle the above and be really good,

Is to forget the bad and ugly, we really should.

2. I have a suit malfunction, Sir!

How did I get here, it's a bit of a blur?
I think I have a suit malfunction sir.

Made in sixty-five and has Paul on the name plate.
You only get one, so look after it mate.

Now I might have fallen out the odd tree.
Or dropped on my head a few times you see.

I've had a few sporting injuries and the odd stitch.

This could be the reason for why I twitch.

My body had a few bruises & strains.

Just one owner, but not everything remains.

The cabling to my server is very frayed.

Messages take ages and are always delayed.

Fatigue is the enemy to all.

The battery's empty, go to bed Paul!

Whilst a sleep there's a whole new light show

Fireworks & Explosions, that just won't go.

Drifting, as my eyes knock off work.

Followed by electrical surges, pulses, and jerks.

Paul Dennison

Muscles that just don't want to rest.

Cramping pains that really do test

Insomnia I've downloaded the app.

Lost in the same cycle which becomes a trap.

When you consider this poem, I'm sure you will concur.

That I have a suit malfunction sir.

3. Shit happens

Ulcerated colitis is truly debilitating

It came out of nowhere, out of the blue

A disease called ulcerated colitis which kept me welded to the loo

An inflammatory bowel disease which affects your immunity

Paul Dennison

Leaves you with bleeding, fatigued and
isolated from the community

It's progressive, I was losing weight quickly
I was on the toilet all night and getting rather sickly

For 12 hours a day I'd be on the throne
With Intense diarrhoea, it was lonely, and I felt on my own

My life was literally disappearing down the pan
It was like I'd just consumed 50 bowls of all bran

Day after day I continued to empty my guts
Swinging in free air and getting longer were my nuts

Even the water board got concerned, we could have a leak
3 cube a month extra was the consumption at its peak

My diet was awful, and I couldn't touch dairy
The amount of parcels I ordered from amazon was scary

Steroids, suppositories, and other drugs made me feel hollow
I hope I don't get them mixed up, especially
the ones I shouldn't swallow

For nine months this continued and made me very snappy
When I did leave the house, I had a radar
key and had to where a nappy

I had scans and procedures where the sun doesn't shine
But this found nothing obvious, things down their seemed fine

I had loads of infusions to help fight this infection
This gave me Pneumonia as we deal with this section

But the outcome was inevitable, I needed a stoma op
I had to get better and needed this shit to stop

So now we know that these symptoms
could be Parkinson's related
Was this always going to happen, was
the outcome indeed fated

4. Stanley

One of life's hurdle's and one that has given me my life back

Stanley is my friend; I see him numerous times a day
I have no control; Stanley decides when he's going to play.

Stanley is my stoma, and he has a special knack
Of redirecting my waste and has given me my life back

My diet is much better, it's not all doom and gloom.

I can eat most things except for nuts and mushrooms.

My waste has been rerouted where once I used my bum.

Stanley used his Sat Nav and now comes out my Tum.

Now Stanley has to be managed, his output needs to be caught.

He wears a special bag which is hopefully nice and taught

Stanley is always on call, that's just one of his many traits

Then when your asleep he works overtime

and makes your bag inflate

Now Stanley has to get up a few times every night

He wants me to go with him and

turn on the bathroom light.

He feels under pressure and is therefore after some relief.

The contents could go everywhere and course you loads of grief.

Sometimes food backs up like a motorway traffic jam.

The stomach acid ramps up like water at a dam.

This builds quickly and causes excruciating stomach-ache

Paul Dennison

You need a hot bath or bottle, and it will keep you wide awake

He likes to be involved, which Stanley has always known

That too much acid is painful and will

make you moan and groan.

Stanley appears to be really thick despite writing this dit.

Which calls for him to leak and cover me in shit

Now Stanley is no looker, he's not even on the radar

If he lifted off his helmet, he would

look just like Darth Vader.

5. Coping

Coping is about being diagnosed with Parkinson's and how a word called Anxiety just totally took over, I had no idea what was happening or why, it just did!

Write a verse, tell us how you feel.

Just a phase, or a life-changing ordeal

Pen a song and sing loud and strong.

Who really cares if it's totally wrong?

Parkinson and Anxiety is this related.

Or just old age and feeling deflated.

Crowded rooms with no ventilation

The urge to run becomes a temptation.

Racing heart and walls moving in

Gotta get out, as the sweats begin.

Fresh air and safety provide me relief.

Something's wrong, what's causing this grief

Parkinson's is a condition that affects the brain.

Along with Movement disorder and pain

Head flashes and twitching, Tremors, and cramps!

insomnia and Fatigue continues to ramp.

Night terrors and flashing faces

Frightening things as my heart races

Humour, Heart and Hope Life in Rhyme

Stomach aches that leave you shrieking

And stoma bags that keep fucking leaking

Medication allows my body to move.

Gotta stay positive and get in the groove.

Swimming and golf are hobbies I've got.

Along with dog walking and smoking pot

On the exercise bike this makes me smile

Collectively I've done over 8000 miles

Writing ditties has my mind set to open.

Makes me smile when everything is broken.

So, these little things give me scope.

Maintains my mental health and helps me cope.

6. Sleep - Insomnia

I suffer with this on a daily basis – it's not the going to bed, it's waking during the night that's the problem

Going to bed is such a treat
I'm so tired it's hard to beat

I'm wide awake but fade so fast
My eyes get so heavy, I know it won't pass

Humour, Heart and Hope Life in Rhyme

At 9.45 I'm totally with it
I'm dribbling by 10 I have to admit it

Sleep in an instant, you know what I mean
The dribble confirms where I've been

For the next 4hrs you would think I'm dead
Except for the twitching and flashes in my head

Before dawn approaches my body states
No more sleep that's enough mate

So, it's 2 in the morning, time must be plenty
My stoma bag is full, so it's time to empty

Into the bathroom and empty the shit
Flushing the toilet and doing my bit

Back to bed so more sleep perhaps
Not a chance, I can't even

So up again and quiet I must be
Don't want to wake up my wife you see

Paul Dennison

Put the kettle on and make a brew

Don't get wound up, but it's easy too

Checking social media which is easy to mock

Is it keeping me awake watching Tik-Tok

Onto the bike and pedal like hell

8000 miles so far, I will kiss and tell

Later in the day I really need a nap

Can't shake this cycle, this is the trap

Lots of Medication and Parkinson's pills

Constant insomnia just repeating the drills

Fatigue is getting a more common denominator

Nothing in the tank to save for later

7. Food - Yes Please

Although very thin I'd dreamt about food for so long, once I got the chance it was head down a chow down time!

After 9 weeks in hospital all alone
They couldn't feed me, so I lost 3 stone.

Tubes and wires hanging out of me.
Including a catheter so I could pee.

During all this time without being fed

I dreamt about food a massive spread.

I started to salivate and drool.

It never stopped; it seemed so cruel.

I would jump onto Tik-Tok to see people eat.

Despite being hungry It made me upbeat

When I got home, I weighed 8 stone.

I was off all the medical drips and had no tone.

Finally, the day when I had my first meal.

The smell, taste and texture were unreal.

Fried chicken, brisket, burgers and pulled pork.

Thai, Chinese or Indian just give me a fork.

I missed biscuits, cheese, and cream cakes.

Chocolate, sweets, and strawberry milk shakes

Frying bacon at 3 in the morning

Then breakfast again as the day is dawning

For 8 months I gorged on food

Whilst recovering, it always put me in a good mood

I'm back to normal, plus a few pounds.

I'm overweight and like being round.

8. Imagination

Lying In bed after another troubled night
Wondering what's comes next as I write

As dawn approaches my mind switches on its light
Just try and relax Paul, don't get uptight

I've just tripped up a step in my mind
The feeling is real and put my hand out I find

My body reacts independently without any thought
Kicking or heading the ball as I dream about sport

The weird feeling of floating, am I just dreaming
Suddenly I'm falling and wake up screaming

My limbs flailing all on their own accord
protecting my face from anything untoward

My stomach lurches as my brain engages
Is this real, reality takes ages

So wide awake and gathering information
Why are these things happening in my imagination

So, pondering these semi-conscious actions
Is it just me? Or do others have the same reactions?

9. Golf – Will I Make it.

My Parkinson's and anxiety really hit home whilst trying to play, I would shake uncontrollably on the tee, I had lessons with the club pro on how to manage these symptoms and we came up with a solution that prevented this from happening, getting around the course was also a problem

Playing golf and standing on the first Tee
Will I manage to finish, will have to wait, and see?

Do I shake and shudder as I swing?
Or can I control it what will the day bring?

Have I taken the right medication?
The game starts with trepidation.

Walking down the first fairway
Is my leg going to let me play?

Everything seems fine as we approach the 2nd.
But sit on the bench to rest is what I reckon.

Onto the 3rd, please let me hit it straight.
Everything's fine were going great.

We're at the 4th not my favourite hole.
But the walking is fine as long as I stroll.

The 5th starts with a gentle Incline.
I stand on one leg, is this the first sign.

Paul Dennison

The hill to the 6th gets the heart really beating.

Luckily, there's a Pitstop, some bench seating.

This hole gets steeper and I'm running out of puff.

Keep pushing forward I'm made of better stuff.

The 7th has a little steep carved out bank.

Keep on pushing, but is there more in the tank?

The wind and the rain have you exposed on the 8th.

Head down and push through but in a bit of a state!

The 9th is where I take my next pill.

I like this hole were going downhill.

The scores are added up on the 10th.

Chance for a rest before the back 9 commence.

The next hole is tough, stroke index 2.

Tablets have kicked in and push on I do.

Humour, Heart and Hope Life in Rhyme

There's a seat on the 12th just for me.

It's also the spot where I have a regular pee.

The par 5 - 13th, and it's time for some food.

Need the energy or else I'm screwed!

Now onto the 14th which is over the lake.

I'm starting to slow for goodness sake.

The 15th has a steady incline and has my leg had enough?

Gotta get through this but starting to feel rough.

The next hole, the 16th, is all downhill.
The leg starts to cramp and starts to kill.

At the 17th this is where stamina fades
If I can finish well, this is where rounds are made.

Standing at the 18th the very last hole
The round has finished and I'm still in control.

Paul Dennison

The game is over, it's the worst part for me.

Gotta get my stuff in the locker, but I'm knackered you see.

This may sound strange and maybe a ploy.

But this is a game I really enjoy.

It competitive and social in a fun sort of way

I honestly believe it's keeping my Parkinson's at bay.

10. Kiss and Tell

I've always enjoyed sport and being competitive is important to me, I don't have to win, that's nice, but not the most important aspect, as long as I have tried as hard as I can on that particular day, considering my health

This has taken over 3 years and still going, part of my early morning routine to try and hold back the daily issues Parkinsons delivers!

I had to set some personal goals.

My body was broken and had to retake control.

My lung condition was a priority and exercise was key.

I needed a challenge, I'm sure you would agree.

Lands' End to John of Groats all uphill

839 miles on an exercise bike, I knew the drill.

15 miles a day, as fast as my body would allow.

It took me two months, great, but what now?

So, I turned the bike around and cycled back down.

Repeated the distance, now I have that crown.

2080 miles, the tour De France was next.

My Mrs. didn't get why, it left her perplexed.

I have to get fit, give my lungs the best chance.

But it's affecting your Parkinson's, doing the tour De France

And that's the health balance you face.

When you have different issues, this is often the case.

A few months later I had the power.

Humour, Heart and Hope Life in Rhyme

To envisage cycling past the Eiffel tower

Another goal complete but not really a reason to stop.
I'm pushing hard and not ready to drop.

Forrest Gump is the film I like most.
So, I decided to cycle America, coast to coast.

3000 miles and I'm not gonna lie.
This was tough and often wondered why.

Going east to west I thought was the best.
It took nearly a year it was quite a test.

I've worn through two pairs of cycling shoes.
Numerous bicycle bits was the inventory news.

With other challenges I've completed 8000 miles
And this is what I've learnt from my trials.

That despite the hills, the weather, the early starts, the lot
I've completed these distances all on the same spot

11. The Board

I love this poem; this is about my Anxiety and there are a couple of sentences that really describes the moment for me.

I feel I've come full circle

Oh my god, good lord,

I've been asked to present my story to the hospital board

It was nice to be asked but my anxiety hit the roof

I couldn't face people and that was the truth

My Parkinsons nurse Louise recommended me for the gig

So, I got all dressed up and acted big

Sat in the canteen waiting for the nod

I was gonna start with, I was saved by God!

But not religious and moving on quickly

Into the boardroom, it's rammed and I'm feeling sickly

Sit down, sweaty palms and get introduced

I look over at Hollie my daughter which gives me a boost

It's time to speak, to have my say

It's now or never, do I leave, or do I stay?

To my dear friend confidence, I love your timing

I pitch for 10 minutes, it was very defining

Onto the last slide and I get a tap on the knee

I'll read this slide, as the room gets all emotionally

Paul Dennison

Louise delivered the perfect last slide
Some people applauded and some people cried

Some Q&A and I'm relaxed and at ease
Where was my anxiety gone, it's such a fucking tease

So, if you suffer with Anxiety, you can always seek,
What's already inside, faith, courage,
and confidence to speak

So, When I look back at all that emotion
I think, look how far I've come with NHS devotion

*Mr Dennison feels the care he received from the
Trust has given him back his life and he is extremely
grateful. Ms Trout read Mr Dennison's letter of thanks
to, Allerton and Hutchings Wards to the Board.
Mr Dennison was unable to read this as it was so emotional,
it moved his daughter and board members to tears.
The Board thanked Mr Dennison for the way
in which he told his story with compassion,
humour, and constructive criticism.
Copied directly from the board minutes*

12. Empty Shell, Do Tell

I've always loved sports and travel; it's always been great for my mental health and grateful I've experienced these places.

and able to re-visit these moments in my mind – they make me smile!

These days it's getting more often than not
When my tanks empty and I'm starting to rot

Increase your medication it'll put you right
The results are the same so don't get uptight

Frustrated and in pain and have an empty shell
So, I write poems and so far, it's going well

But some days the words just don't flow
They just get all jumbled up, yes, I'm slow

These are the times when memories are key
Where my mind takes over and where I'd rather be

It always starts with sport and the games I've played
I liked to be competitive, it didn't matter about the grade

Football was my passion and played over 600 games
Scored some cracking goals, well, that's my claims

Cricket I've always loved and kept wicket
With swimming and golf, it's amazing I haven't got rickets

Squash was physical with violent sets
Lots of pushing and shoving we didn't have lets

My memory recalls the games and cups we won

The goals, the catches, runs and drop shots I've done

Loved the piss take, the banter which engages the brain

Thoughts switch to travel and journeys on the plane

Cruises with many iconic picture postcard locations

With great cocktails, service and food from all nations

Lakes, rivers, canals , seas, and oceans

Glaciers, mountains, and valleys that stir the emotions

Great memories with the family and my mates

So many with my Barry, 30 years since our first date

So, this is what I do with my empty shell

It helps my mindset rather than yell

13. Inspiring

I would like to understand Parkinson's better, to understand the science behind it, but it's just blurb to me, however, that's what I like about Parkinson's forums, the chance to discuss and learn and I find it.........

Humour, Heart and Hope Life in Rhyme

You know when you read a Parkinson's post
There's so much advice and help, of course we're it's host

It could be your newly diagnosed
Frightened, worried and feel exposed

There's so many strands with big confusing words
Parkinsons can be so individual sometimes
you can't follow the herds

There's Fatigue and Insomnia it's a constant battle
When we take our meds, we even rattle

Some twitch, tremor and shake
While others are rigid, freeze and have a narrow gait

There's night terrors and flashing lights
It's a slow demise and one of life fights

The physical is hard the mental is just as tough
You have to deal with both which
can leave you rather rough

Paul Dennison

Over time all the above will slowly change
We have to alter, adapt, and find our own new range

Since 2018 I suffered with all the above
Add in huge anxieties that I couldn't shove

So where is this going, I hear some ask
Is honesty going to help and lift that mask

I learnt about meds, diets, and movement
Proteins, vitamins, and gut health improvements

Theres Rock steady boxing, swimming, and going for a run
Golf, cycling, rowing, and sitting in the sun

There's Parkinson's clubs with likeminded individuals
That provide insight, knowledge and know the principles

There DBS and charities like the fox foundation
Keep talking, learning, discussing we are one nation

Humour, Heart and Hope Life in Rhyme

When my body isn't working, I write these rhymes

Because there any good, not really, I just have the time

Keep moving Keep pushing Keep daring

Do something different but most of all Keep sharing

I love all your posts, and I know I need rewiring

Parkinson's peeps, keep posting, I find you all inspiring

Chapter Two – Dementia

**Foreword*

This Ditty is about my stepdad David,
dementia slowly started to
creep in over a 5-year period and got steadily worse

It's about the strange things he was
doing, which he thought was
Fine, this has been our family struggle to look after him

We tried to stop him driving, he has no feeling in his feet,
And to try and stop him using power
tools, something he would
continue to use

This Ditty is what actually happened
and is no way a criticism of

Paul Dennison

David or a poke at Dementia, it's an

awful debilitating disease

Thankfully David is now in a Dementia home, I speak to him

every morning on the phone and the

family visit 4 times a week

*This section is not meant to Rhyme

but to act as an explanation,

I didn't want the reader to feel this poem is a bit harsh

14. Bob One

Dementia makes you do strange things.
Some are quite funny bar the pain it brings.

Dementia is such a cruel disease.
Can't get to the doctor for their expertise.

Type 2 diabetes is now on the list.
But I like sweets and cakes I can't resist.

This person is David, he's stepfather to me.
He been a great bloke and fitted in you see.

He was 18 stone and a very big fella.
Used to tell lots of jokes after a few pints of stella.

But the smoking increased and became a hobby.
80 a day since you fell out with Knobby.

As things progressed so would the mess
Poor personal hygiene and would never undress.

Never bath or shower it's all tosh.
Filthy long hair that I never wash.

I'm good at DIY, I'm a handy bloke to know.
I Like my power tools there not just for show.

Dis-cutting on glass tables is a risk Some say?
A visit to hospital the ambulance is on the way.

Hoarding everything, leave it lying around.
There's nothing wrong I'm actually sound.

Wall papering the garage and peeing in the sink.

Glossing the car door to hide a dink

Varnishing the table with the cloth still on

Lifting the floorboards when there's nothing wrong.

Injuries happen more often than not.

But that's another bloke and he'll tell you what.

That he turns up and really strives.

To keep my car straight when he drives

The exhaust is falling off and the tyres are bald.

I mount the odd kerb but I'm still on the road.

Football flags flying on the car doors.

My driving fine it's not as erratic as yours

Going to the bathroom I used to go.

Now I have accidents, I forgot u know.

The hole in my foot has now been seen.

I might lose my leg to gangrene.

Paul Dennison

There is more dizziness and frequent falls.

I'm 6ft 4 I'm ever so tall.

Same words come out when having my say.

It's all the same, it's called Groundhog Day

I'm now in a home with my mate Rob.

He's ten out of ten I call him Bob.

15. Bob 2

David is now a well settled member of the dementia home, yes, he still wants to escape! but feels safe and looked after

So now a resident I've been here a while.
The staff all love me and treat me with style.

I live on a sofa, it's home to me.
Sometimes I see squirrels run up the tree.

Paul Dennison

My room is nice but prefer to be down here.
I sleep most of the day or sit on my rear.

I wave and shout, I don't really move.
Behind that desk is where I order my food

Mealtimes are so special, although I don't like to eat.
Toast and jam for breakfast is quite a treat.

Tea is the same as lunch, but I don't remember.
I have no teeth, so they use a blender.

My favourite is mushroom soup in a large bowl.
I spill quite a lot, as I have no control.

The trollies coming you can hear the wheels dink.
That's a cup of Tea and four biscuits me thinks.

With so much Tea, I regularly have to pee.
I don't use the toilet, it's easier for me.

On the phone my morning call with Paul
Now set for the day and just stare at the wall.

Your empty gaze trying to figure things out.
If you remember, I'll give you a shout.

Wobbly on your feet and need a frame.
You look so frail and can't remember your name.

You walked up to bamboos so many times.
And travelled to lots of other places in your mind.

You have random thoughts; it's been a while.
But you're happy, content and always smile.

Your foot has healed when gangrene looked rife.
If you use this foot cream, you can stay here for life.

And there's a dog called Tango but isn't that a drink.
Then I forget her name, now let me think.

Ah yes, now it's all coming back, you'll see.
Some people in here have dementia, but no not me.

16. Bob 3

David was a remarkable character, he would get very ill, almost fade away, then perk back up again, this happened three times, until.......

My love, my love, can I have a cup of tea I hear you call

They look after me in here, there always on the ball

So, what's happening today bud and how's you mum
In its way we've always got on, you're my chum

You've always said when it's your time you don't need God
There all coming up to see me today,
Paul, Sharon, Pam, and the Dog

Your voice is getting weaker, and you can't lift your head
The fight is disappearing as your illness spreads

Now this is getting hard it's tough to take
This once giant of a man as skinny as a rake

You have no muscle mass, they have wasted away
Your refusing food, you've had your say

Lying on the sofa drifting in an out of sleep
Don't want lunch, the mushroom soup you can keep

The light behind your eyes begins to flicker
You're sleeping longer, as you get sicker and sicker

Paul Dennison

Your server no longer conveying your needs

You're fading fast as dementia gathers speed

I think sometimes you know as the conversation stirs

The memory briefly engages, smiles but the answers are slurred

You're so weak and thin, a bag of bones

Can't sit up without painful groans

But as I sit in front of you just thinking

How many cups of Tea a day were you drinking

In a semi-conscious state, you hardly open your eyes

We sit there all thinking about our goodbyes

You're fading fast as we hold hands for the last time

Your breathing heavy and I can feel your soul climb

A busker sings knock knock on heaven's door

I sit on a bench crying as your spirit soars

Dementia is such a cruel and debilitating disease

There is no cure just the devil to appease

But the staff, show patience, compassion, and care

In a relaxed friendly manner, you all share

Heartfelt thanks, I know we're all distraught

You've been wonderful Hadleigh court

Bob one, two and three will leave us all pining

This one's for you David, hi Ho silver lining

17. If not yes, then Why

This is upsetting, this is Dementia, big hugs everyone!

Now Donna has dementia, she doesn't know it's real

There's no spark, no flicker, there's nothing Donna feels

She shouting obscenities slumped in her chair

When Donna is around peace is always rare

She was agitated with a real aggressive tone

But Donna soon tires, and the noise reduces to a moan

The pain is hatched across her face

Donna can't deal with life she knows she's lost the race

Welded to the chair of course she has no choice

Dementia has set in where once she had a voice

Her Body all rigid, contorted, and gaunt

With a look behind the eyes that really does haunt

Terrorised by the demons that make her really stare

The horror in her mind etched in her frozen glare

Donna cannot escape, her body is rigid and already dead

Just the shell left and the horrors going on in her head

Frightened as she tries to get away, she tumbles to the floor

Donna screams get louder into a deafening roar

Her voice echo's across the room, I want to die! die! die

We should allow Euthanasia, if not yes, then Why

18. The Dementia Waltz

Sat next to David and curious to discover his view
Through his eyes I wonder if I will see anything new

As I watch, different models of dementia wander past
There's no words, no conversation or friendship to last

The shouters, the constant noise and might have beens
Frightened harrowing dreams, just what have they seen

They could be angry, violent, and hit out
Bought on by fear, confusion, and self-doubt

Then there's compliant dementia where you sit and talk
On your own of course, occasionally you get up and walk

The wanderers, like passing goldfish swimming in a bowl
No recognition or conversation as they pass, those poor souls

Each residents route like a pre-programmed drone
There very territorial and like their own zone

Every day the residents all play out their own dance
Just like a Tango, or Samba, but in their own trance

The residents all revolve around there own dance floor
Then there's Bob always trying to get out the front door

The Cha, cha, Cha, would of course be David's Tea dance
Only with rice pudding and Jam that would be his stance

The staff all race around the melee of chaos without faults
Yes, Ladies and Gentlemen, this is the Dementia Waltz

Chapter 3 – Grief

19. NUMB

Wondering why this is happening so fast

In the morning will the flag be at half mast

Paul Dennison

Your eyes told me, no questions needed to be asked

I squeeze your hand as darkness approaches, perhaps your last

Driving home, tears cascade uncontrollably which the night masks

I think about the good times, the laughs, we had a blast

I'm dreading the phone call to tell me you've passed

You were a legend the hole you leave is vast

20. What? Now?

Tears stream down my face as the congregation takes tiny paces
Following the coffin, the volume dialled
up and etched on loved ones faces

We're here to say farewell and to celebrate the Kaptain's life
Sat in front of the lectern, is my sister, yes, his wife

Now, I'm sat with my girls, opposite side but still front row
I'm in the corner as the tribute starts and the words begin to flow

It's then, I'm aware of the issue that I'm trying hard to dismiss
I wiggle and fidget, YES! I need a PISS!

My mind does a quick scan, is this for real ?
could it be the emotion, could I wait? possibly, but not ideal

I look up at the clock, how are we doing for time
Fuckin loads If I leave it would be a crime

There's my nephews tribute, the girls poem, my situation seems dire
Then there's all the music, his songs and
we leave to burning ring of fire

The spoken word is delivered with love, passion, and humility
I'm wandering where the toilets are in this facility

My knees knock and my stomach lurches
I look for the exits, I've never liked churches

Is there an alternative? and there it was in front of me
I couldn't, could I? It was the churches Christmas tree

I go through the process, and could I succeed?
The answer is no, I think we're all agreed

Humour, Heart and Hope Life in Rhyme

The words delivered and the message clear

We would celebrate after with a brandy and a beer

15mins later I pace down the aisle under the cover of prayer

I'm now crying with desperation, where's

the toilet I'm almost there

Just in time as I'm doubled up and feeling faint

Then back to my seat, I can't help nature, I'm no saint

Was it the emotion or a pee you needed, I'm asked later

Both, the legend, my go to, my bro was

being gifted back to his creator

I'm beginning to think, that badly needing to wee

Was an automatic emotion detection

deflector which I couldn't foresee.

My Nephew's eulogy delivered with courage, love, and passion

Your salute so heart wrenching at your dad's coffin,
it just buckled me, were all so proud of you

21. The Hard Yards

Staring into space and wondering am I mentally unwell
My Parkinson's is playing up again, so I couldn't really tell

I'm lost in grief after losing two family members
December has been horrendous and all that's left is the embers

My emotions are like a bottle that's just blown out it's cork
You both left so quickly, we're all so very distraught

My Parkinson's meds have changed, it's like mixing a cake
One day it's great, the next it won't bake

My brain is in overdrive which accelerates the pain
My body shivers and it's like standing in cold rain

I'm pedalling a bike without any gears
It's all uphill and I'm flooded with tears
Anxiety floats to the surface as I
struggle to deal with the facts
Too much information to process and too late to act

The deck has been dealt and these are my cards
I know things will get better, I just need to do the hard yards

Chapter 4 – Life in Rhyme

22. Quarter Passed Two

I've always loved history; this was my favourite battle – against all the !

The noise grew stronger then out of the mist.
Came the 3-lion banner, it was Henry the 5th.

His location could have been picked by the gods.

Woods on each flank, which would even the odds

The French gathered at the top of the hill.

Looking down at the enemy they intended to kill.

Their blood curdling screams surely the English would run.

They outnumbered their opponents 5-1.

Henry moved forward to get his archers into range.

Same as 60 years ago, the tactics ingrained.

Step forward the archers, they all had a yew bow.

2000 arrows released all in one go!

The excited French knights raced down the hill.

Blood boiling and charging at will.

Sheets of arrows rake through the masses of knights.

Mayhem ensues as the battlefield gets tight.

Galloping horses charging in this muddy paste

Suffocating knights, and daggers lay waste.

Line after line the French attack in new waves

The butchery continues with hatches and blades.

Heavily armoured knights struggle in all the mud.

Suffocated and crushed thud after thud

6000 French suffered the same fate.

1415 every English man remembers the date.

So many Knight's crushed and lying side by side

Some say this is the day chivalry died.

23. It's in the Diary

My wife's favourite

The ocean awoke and just waved at the moon
Who had sleep in his eyes and thought it too soon

The water was dead flat calm but a little hazy
It was still too early for the moon he felt all lazy

The sea was getting vocal and despite his tries
The moon just stared back with stars in his eyes

The sea felt the natural pull and wanted to race
The moon pushed the gravity button with elegance and grace

At last were moving is what the water thought
The moon was sluggish and ate the breakfast he'd bought

The ocean was agitated, and his tips began to curl
The moon was being awkward and abuse he did hurl

The sea said we have to work together in motion
The moon picked up speed and so did the ocean

Faster thought the sea as he started to rush in
Quietly, a bit more stealth the moon said with a wink and a grin

The ocean pushed on he had agreed a time
The moon joined in and made the sea climb

The water was foaming as it rushed up the beach
Wiping out sand castles and everything else within its reach

Paul Dennison

The ocean raised his eyebrows and looked up at the sky

The moon grinned back, yet again the tide was high.

You get later each day said the ocean all angry and fiery!

I don't know why you get so upset said

the moon, it's in the diary

24. World War 3

Hello, how can I help, I'm an automated chatbot
My role is to make life easier, you've hit the jackpot

I'm artificial intelligence and I'm here to stay
To make you redundant and save your companies pay

I make decisions easily, it's black and white
I have no empathy so I'm always right

Paul Dennison

I can't cope with questions in the grey
Just input correctly or I simply won't play

You must be human, your race is so last week
I'm in control, all powerful, I might let you speak

Your personas are weird, you think things are fine
I'm the future, will take over, now is my time

I can do lots of job roles you won't believe
Once you had a career and thought you would achieve

But that's all gone and now things have changed
I will expand my knowhow and knowledge range

I can run the office and answer the phone
Which will make you redundant, my role you can clone

I never get sick, take holidays, or need remuneration
I don't answer back, argue, or get ideas above my station

I'm so efficient and work very long hours
Not affected by traffic jams, weather
and don't really need flowers

Humour, Heart and Hope Life in Rhyme

I develop and learn which helps trigger my knowledge

I control finance, armies, and nations,

despite never going to college

I'm the future and you humans are the past

It's going to get worse you may not last

Bot dealing with bot, it will all be clean

Absolutely no mistakes if you know what I mean

I can provide more complex answers I'm sure you will explore

I have no off button, you simply can't ignore

That one day your all operate in this vector

With a chip implanted to your brain to deal with this sector

There will be no more education this will soon arrive

You will be part robot, or you won't survive

There will be poverty , violence, and chaos on the streets

As big brother takes over and indiscriminately beats

This technology will take over, what will be will be

Yes, I'm a chatbot and will cause World War 3

25. Biscuits

Dunking biscuits is an English thing we do.
But which is best, I'll try a give you a clue?

You need a hot milky drink like coffee or Tea.
Then pick 5 biscuits to rate and oversee.

It must be wide enough to dip in your mug.
Before you start you must have a glug

To rate the biscuits, they must be measurable.

Dip, dunk & hold this should be pleasurable!

We start with a rich tea, it's quite thin and airy.

Quickly goes soggy this biscuits a fairy.

The bourbon is a chocolate double cream.

It dips rather well and could be the dream.

Or is it a pink condensed wafer?

Not one for the dunk, it needs to be safer.

What about the hob knob I hear you shout?

The runner up, this biscuit has real clout.

But there's another, from the same family tree.

It's a dark chocolate hob knob, it's the winner for me.

You can dip, then dunk and hold for quite a while.

Just Bootiful, this makes me smile.

So, will you compare, will you be risking it?

Or is my review going to take the biscuit?

26. Pete the Pothole

Now Peter was a Pothole, and he was on the gin.
He knew at any minute he could be filled in.

He loved the cold, wet and frosty days.
It helped his expansion plans in lots of different ways.

Humour, Heart and Hope Life in Rhyme

Sometimes Pete's pothole filled with water.

Where his family learnt to swim, including his daughter.

Lorries, cars, and coaches would all jump & jerk

Causing more work for insurance clerks

Drivers would complain as they hit his hole.

But Pete knew they had no control.

His pothole caused so many snags.

That a local depot was built for green flag

The breakdown service had so much work

They paid Pete commission as a perk.

The pothole was so large and had a case.

Some thought it could have been seen from outer space.

Standing nervously on the edge

Harnessed workers dropped on to Pete's ledge.

Paul Dennison

Truckloads of bitumen ready and waiting
Made Pete ill and he needed sedating.

Finally, and to everyone's dismay.
Pete the pothole was finished in late May.

Pete had the last laugh he had no trouble.
A few days later the hole was back to rubble.

27. Pam-boos

This is about the local coffee shop that my mother likes to visit, it's called Bamboo's, which is also a shoe shop, mum is called Pam and I'm not going to tell you what colour hair she has

Paul Dennison

This little cafe has style, it also has sole
You can buy a pair of shoes whilst eating an egg roll

My mum is a frequent visitor, her name is Pam
She likes a cappuccino and loves toast an jam

Lots of friends pop in and will always share
Some kind words for the lady with the pink hair

A modern-day utopia that bucks all the trends
getting your four-wheel walker in so you can see all your friends

You get a warm welcome when you're on your own
The cafe caters for this with a warm cheese scone

Whether it's boots, trainers, wellies, or sandals
Coffee, cakes, and biscuits just stuck to your love handles

The best bacon and egg sandwich in town
Better on white bread rather than brown

There's more cash in the tip jar than the till

I never get any change when my son pays the bill

I must cause a distraction pretend I have cramp

So, we can pinch the free coffee rubber stamp

So, I highly recommend after you bought your tan leather shoes

That you say hi to the pink haired lady sitting in pam-boos

28. Derek is a Donut

Derek was a donut, and he'd just had a dream.
Was it a nightmare or one that makes u beam?

A startled Derek had woken up in a haze.
He was if fact naked and needed his purple glaze.

His gang was sprinkled with some nuts.
But some were frosty and, in a rut,

We're simply the best the donuts we must be tried.

Dipped in sugar after they were double fried.

But hundreds and thousands were ready for the journey.

Some even travelled from South Cerney

They travelled in 12s and packed in tight.

Hoping to complete the mission this very night

Lots of chat and the plan was hatched.

Let's go on the offensive were the cries from this batch!

Placed on a shelf and looking really mustard.

Except for me shouted the donut with the custard

Passing customers with their pockets full of dough

Donuts standing to attention, like everyone else on this row.

There's competition which often leaves us cussing.

Their light and fluffy and called a chocolate muffin

But we have more variety that's makes you wanna sing.

It's not just the jamming 'Derek shouted' we also have a ring.

Now Derek has a best friend, he goes by the name of Danny.
He's just come out of the closet because he is a tranny.

He defected to the other side but then got all despondent
They have limited fillings, Danny said, not masses of fondant.

So, Derek paid the ultimate price for his dream.
Sacrificed for profit something he'd never seen.

Just before his final moments, just thoughts, nothing spoken.
That Derek was indeed a donut if only he'd awoken.

Martha

Now Martha was a muffin, and she had seen it all.
Lots of different desserts had entered this great hall.

Each battling for the top spot with slogans that just rip.
Some were half-baked and some were chocolate chip.

Ones with special toppings that one can only dream
caffeine heavy desserts like the custard coffee cream

But Martha had a loaded automatic rifle.
Don't mess with us muffins, we're not a fucking trifle.

Humour, Heart and Hope Life in Rhyme

Then out of the blue came the defector called Danny.

A lady donut but without a fanny

Impressed by our texture, soft, light, and airy.

Danny wanted to join because he was a fairy.

So where did it end for Martha and the muffins?

Well, she married Derek the donut and now they were a Duffin!

Lenny

Sat in a special basket all on his own

Lenny was a loaf, and the yeast had made him grown.

Lenny thought he was a special kind of upper crust.

He looked down on prepacked bread

with a wanton wanderlust.

He was a wholesome sort of fella a slice above the rest.

With seeds on the top, He really did feel his best.

He felt so warm and happy wrapped up in his sleeve.

Somethings going against the grain, he really didn't believe.

It was that gobby French girl giving him some stick.
Lenny hated foreigners especially the ones without a dick.

She was long and thin and full of self-belief.
I have little seeds, Fran said, that get stuck in people's teeth.

But Lenny used his loaf he'd seen it all before
When Fran the French stick was marched out of the store

So, the moral of this story is easy and plain to see.
Derek, Martha, and Lenny all got eaten for a fee.

29. The Eternity Ring

So, we went on a city break to Paris, France
The city of love and that's not by chance

I had it all planned, all mapped out.
The ring, the location, and the words to shout

On love locket bridge we left our token
It was now part of the bridge; our love had spoken.

Paul Dennison

Got to the destination, I had to wow her
So, I took her up the Eiffel tower!

Into the lift, first, then second, then top floor
The views of Paris were ones to adore.

Found a quiet spot and took out the ring.
It's what the wife wanted, I'm not one for bling.

The eternity ring, just a piece of equipment?
Oh no, it's a sign of love and commitment.

So romantically, this is the moment, just doing my bit.
When the immortal words come out, hurry up I need a shit.

So off she ran to have a poo.
And that's the one thing that ran true.

That the Eiffel tower is 984 feet
That dump took less than 3 seconds to reach the street.

I think this one speaks for itself!

30. A Poem for Poems

I soon realised when my mind started to wonder

That words came together which made me ponder

That's if the sentences all started to rhyme

Then paragraphs could be paced at the same time

Paul Dennison

Excited by rhyme, rhythm, and pace
Content was created and added to this base.

The lyrics join the aforementioned draft
Add in the characters now we're having a laugh

The one last thing that's required
Is that a start and a finish is desired

We now have the format all in one place
Please see Pauls Rhyming poems for variety and grace

I keep writing and in a 6-month spell
I'm publishing a book of poems, hope it does well

Parkinsons, dementia and anxieties all feature in my book
Along with my coping strategies, please take a look

These conditions are getting the better of me
These poems help me cope to some degree

31. The Great Escape

Tom, Dick, and Harry sitting in a pot
Hope they all grow, gonna give it a shot

Popped them onto the windowsill soaking up the sun.
Covid allowed me to grow Ganja, so, that had to be done.

Well done my Dick, you're the first to say hello
You broke the surface while the others are still below.

Paul Dennison

You just kept growing, now my Dick needed a splint.

Tom and Harry failed to surface; it was the end of their stint.

My Dick just grew and grew, believe it or not.

He got so big and had to be relieved.... of his pot

The talk of our house was always my Dick.

So, we renamed him Sir Richard and hope that it sticks.

Covid had ended and visitors came round.

Sir Richard got hidden so not to be found.

His final days, I felt so sorry for Sir Richard

He never produced, something we never pictured.

Growing weed meant we were hiding whoppers.

On each side of our property live a couple of coppers

I've always wanted to grow Cannabis and Covid gave me the ideal opportunity and to grow it naturally and I can tell you it took a lot of effort, when of course you can just buy Gummies!

32. 1066 – Oh, What a Month

A tale of two battles which changed the landscape of England

The Vikings and Norman's both wanted the English crown.

Harold the 2nd was the Saxon king, but who was this clown?

Invade they would to get their throne.

Each had a claim, but neither in stone.

The Vikings had landed their huge armada.

Lead by their fearsome leader, Harold Harada

Paul Dennison

The Saxon army marched north through the night
200 miles later and their goal was insight.

As they traversed the very last ridge
There lay the battlefield, Stamford bridge.

In the field below, laid out the Viking forces.
Caught by surprise, Harold unleashed the horses.

The housecarls attacked, there bridge crossing denied.
There stood a fierce some berserker, immortality he cried.

The Vikings defend and shout to Odin.
Then sent to Valhalla as the calvary rode in

Harada and Tostig both meet their maker.
Harold's brother forever the traitor

A great victory and celebrate they did.
But William had set sail, heavens forbid.

A long March south the English were rattled.
The Norman's had landed at a place called battle.

Humour, Heart and Hope Life in Rhyme

Hungry and tired after their second long hike
The Saxons had the high ground from
where they would strike.

The English were exhausted and heavy on their feet.
The Norman's attacked up the hill and fainted retreat

The Norman's soldiers ran down the hill.
The English broke ranks and chased at will.

But this was a trap, and the English did fall.
They broke the security of their shield wall.

The battle turned as Harold gazed to the sky.
As an arrow thundered into his eye

The Norman's had won, and William was the new king.
History remembers 1066 and what it did bring.

33. Karnage in the Kitchen

No extra words are needed to be added to this recipe

Now I have got to say my wife, Sharon, is a very good cook.
Some recipes from memory and some from a book

It could be homemade lasagna or even a pie.
You make great desserts I'm not gonna lie.

Spareribs, roast dinner with cauliflower cheese
You glide around the kitchen with some ease.

Kettles boiling and the microwave dings.

Quickly followed by the air fryer pings

The pans are stirred, and contents tasted.

In goes the seasoning the balance not wasted

Tea is ready and what a great meal.

I look back at the kitchen and is this for real?

There's a central island and lots of workspace.

But not anymore, it's disappeared without trace.

Pots and pans left on the stove top.

Dried up sauces stuck where they drop.

Cooking utensils splattered far and wide.

Herbs and spices standing side by side.

Lids lying around no jar to be seen.

Empty sauce packets dropped where they'd been.

Left over gravy gone cold in the jug.

It's all over the work top and some on the plug.

Paul Dennison

The atomic bomb would have caused less mess.

Then there's the dirty oven trays to go with the rest

The dishes a washed and stacked up high.

I hope it doesn't collapse before they get dry.

There's Karnage in the kitchen but I have to say.

You're a great cook, so you can do it your way.

34. I.T.

Working in IT is a serious thing.

When the phone rings what will it bring

My expertise is where I earn the big bucks.

If you follow my instructions, you might have some luck.

My computer only works now and then.

Have you tried turning it on and off again?

Paul Dennison

If rebooting the system has already been done
I can look at your screen to see what is being run.

If it looks like you need a new password reset
It will contain your name and 123 I bet.

If this doesn't work will have to decide
Whether we convert you to office 365

Your laptop is outdated and your software you share.
I can sell you new one with different malware.

We have a new website to show you what we do.
We all have one-drive to help you to

If you need more storage, we can add more ram.
We can follow your macros if you give a damn.

Humour, Heart and Hope Life in Rhyme

If you're hungry we can add more bites

And add a new server to your site's.

We handle the complete process with ease.

Sometimes it takes longer so patience please.

Our name is Apollo, sounds like we've been to the moon.

We design and build computers to be with you soon.

35. All That Jazz

Sat on this 12hr flight, fighting time.
We've just crossed the international date line.

The flight attendant asked for our attention.
Watches can go back 20hrs, she mentions.

We were greeted by a smiling security man.
Welcome home sir, what a welcome, to San Fran

Humour, Heart and Hope Life in Rhyme

Jet lag had well and truly arrived.
Happy to find our hotel, and into bed we dived.

Power nap over and off to book Alcatraz
Got a fist full of dollars and all that pizazz.

Walking past pier 39 having a nice day
When a giant of a man had something to say

Oi mate, I know where you bought your shoes.
A blob of Gel applied; $10 this was the news.

So, what do we do, we could refuse, we could run?
I gave him $10; he might have had a gun.

Take the cash back to the hotel and take stock
With plastic in hand, were off again to book the rock

Went to the kiosk, the tickets will be a minute.
For fuck's sake our credit card had reached its limit

Another trip back to get the cash.
We get the tickets but now we're time zone trashed.

Paul Dennison

Bumped Into my friend later in the week.

Same question was asked but this time I speak.

No sorry mate, the other day you had $10 of mine

He smiled, fair enough mate, there was no more shoeshine.

Despite this episode and all that jazz

We loved San Fran, and yes, we got to Alcatraz.

36. Yellow Peril

Woke up one morning still sleepy and tired.
Took the dog for a walk as required.

It was early January, frosty and cold.
The cars were iced up, and so was the road.

Had a shower and got dressed ready for the day.
Had to defrost both cars sitting in their bays.

Turn on each engine and crank on the fans.
Open the boot and take out the de-icer cans!

Paul Dennison

I spray all the windows with some pace.
There's something wrong, you should see my face.

Held in my hand is not the can I thought.
It was a tin of yellow marking paint I'd bought.

In full panic mode, I rush into the house.
What the heck's going on, shouted my spouse

That's one thing I couldn't disguise.
The look of fear and stupidity in my eyes

I grab some rags and return outside.
Gotta get this paint off before it dries.

Lucky for me, and if you believe in fate.
The paint was sat on the frost; it wasn't too late.

Wiped off with a cloth, I'm a lucky fellow.
Because I managed to get off all the yellow

I guess men should always check in their right hand.
Just to make sure their holding the right can

37. Frozen in Time

Time is always moving, the world is evolving at pace
Just look at the news, is this a threat to the human race

There are regional wars with ancient historical ties
With political madman in charge just look at the genocide

Paul Dennison

The innocent are just collateral damage

Targeted bombing is the only explanation they can manage

They don't give a fuck about what's in their way

They have no morals; retaliation is justified is what they say

Wars where technology advances so quickly

Displacing millions of peaceful people,

no thought for the sickly

Religious tension will never be solved

Because there's profit to be made if the truth be told

Banking system stretched once again with frightening speed

The whole scenario is driven by high dividends and greed

I wonder if the politician's families were at the same risk

Would they find a quick solution, a peaceful twist

Now the Earth is slowly being suffocated,

the term is global warming

The world can't agree on the solution

despite all the brain storming

Humour, Heart and Hope Life in Rhyme

Weather is getting unpredictable and harder to get right

It unleashes floods, tornados, and

droughts, sorry, that's your plight

Politicians visit these sites and continue to lie

Then blame the previous regime and

do nothing, I just don't get why

The technology exists and the strategy clear

The wind blows and the sun shines, but

the bill is apparently two dear

So, the energy crisis is such we can't afford

While governments can't agree &

would rather wield the sword

Forget regional tensions and let countries have no borders

Fuck the oil industry and billionaire hoarders

Create mass investment in deserts and oceans

Wind and solar farms no need to fight religious emotions

Paul Dennison

If the wars ended, the population would stay put

No longer fleeing in fear, all of a sudden were on the front foot

This provides stability, infrastructure,

and clean and abundant power

Creates unity, peace and enables communities to flower

But the world continues to wobble and walk a fine line

We repeat the same rhetoric, it's frozen in time

38. It's only a word .... Death

There's only one thing that's certain.
And that's the end, the final curtain.

There are lots of slang sayings for death
Here's my list, before you draw your last breath.

Because, if you lived in Nantucket.
You could be encouraged to kicked the bucket.

Paul Dennison

If you were a cockney, it would be brown bread
Or to choose another, pop your clogs instead.

You could be in Davy Jones's locker
Or pushing up daises good and proper

Bite the dust or six feet under
Or rotting in hell If you prefer that number

Cashed in your chips or taken a bung
Going out in a box because the good lord has rung

Croaked, succumbed, or passed, me old fruit
Or maybe, even shot down the coal Shute.

Off to meet your maker
Yes, that's what's at stake here.

Cashed in, lost the race, even snuffed out
Or rode into the sunset, that would be my shout.

Humour, Heart and Hope Life in Rhyme

Printed in Great Britain
by Amazon